Pascual and the Kitchen Angels

written and illustrated by

TOMIE dePAOLA

G. P. Putnam's Sons   New York

For Eduardo Fernandez—Lalo-Uno—who "introduced" me to San Pascual.

Also for Danny Meyer of Union Square Cafe,
Gramercy Tavern, Eleven Madison Park, Tabla and Blue Smoke.
"The Two Hot Tamales," Mary Sue Milliken and Susan Feniger, of Border Grill and Ciudad.

As well as Judy Rodgers of Zuni Cafe, Alice Waters of Chez Panisse
and Sara Moulton of the Food Network
(none of whom I've met).

And, last but not least, my "FOODIE" friends,
Cecilia Yung, Mary Ann Esposito, Carol Field, Mary Richter and Mario.

All are true Kitchen Angels.

Copyright © 2004 by Tomie dePaola
Published simultaneously in Canada. Manufactured in China by South China Printing Co. Ltd.
Designed by Gina DiMassi and Marikka Tamura. Text set in Raleigh Demi Bold.
The art was done on 140 lb. Arches handmade rough watercolor paper using acrylics and gesso.
Library of Congress Cataloging-in-Publication Data
De Paola, Tomie.   Pascual and the kitchen angels / written and illustrated by Tomie dePaola.   p. cm.
Summary: Pascual, a boy blessed by angels at his birth, receives divine help when the Franciscan monks make him their cook.
[1. Angels—Fiction. 2. Cookery—Fiction. 3. Monasteries—Fiction. 4. Christian life—Fiction.] I. Title.
PZ7.D439Pas 2004   [E]—dc21   2003008521
ISBN 0-399-24214-7
1 3 5 7 9 10 8 6 4 2
First Impression

"Look, everyone! We have a son," Papa said to the villagers.
"Shall we call him Pascual?" Mama asked.

Suddenly, doves swooped down, and the air was filled with song.

"Listen, Mama, the angels are singing for Pascual," Papa said.

"Oh, Papa, those are only the doves from the church tower," Mama said.

"Look again, Mama," Papa said.

Sure enough, the tree was filled with angels. "We have a special little boy," Papa said, smiling. "God must surely love him."

All the animals loved Pascual, too. He was their friend.

One day, Papa said, "Mama, Pascual is singing to the sheep."

"La-la-la," Pascual sang.

"The sheep are singing back to him," Mama said.

"Baa-baa-baa," the sheep sang.

Mama and Papa didn't know that Pascual and the sheep were singing to God.

"I think Pascual is going to be a shepherd," Papa said.

And Pascual was. Every morning, he led the sheep to the fields and watched over them.

If a lamb strayed, he took it back to its mother.

"Stay near your mother, little one," he told the lamb. And it did.

He frolicked with the young ones.

"I can jump higher than you," he told the lambs. And he did.

Every afternoon, Pascual made garlands of flowers and hung them around the necks of the sheep. Then he would kneel and pray to God.

Every evening, Pascual and the sheep sang back and forth to each
other on the way home.

"La-la-la . . ."

"Baa-baa-baa . . ."

As they walked along, Pascual gave cheese he had saved from his
lunch to anyone who was hungry.

One evening, he saw some boys fighting.

"Friends," Pascual said, "take these and be happy!" He put the garlands
around the boys' necks and they stopped fighting.

Papa was watching.

"I think that the angels protect our boy," he told Mama.

Pascual took care of the sheep until he was a young man.

Then he said to Mama and Papa, "I want to be a friar and help feed people who are hungry."

"You must go to the monastery of Saint Francis," they told Pascual.

The next day, Pascual left for the monastery where the Franciscans lived. He carried a basket of cheeses, eggs, flour, dried beans, vegetables and fruit from Mama. It was a gift for the friars.

"Oh, Pascual," the friars said, "look at all the food you brought. You must cook dinner for us tonight."

Poor Pascual! He didn't know how to cook. But he was afraid to tell them. They might not let him stay.

So Pascual went to the kitchen. All the pots and pans, bowls and dishes made his head spin. How did he boil water? How did he cook the beans? How did he make the bread?

Pascual knelt on the stone floor and prayed. Suddenly, there was a swoosh in the air above him. Angels in little white aprons were flying down to cook.

Pascual didn't notice them. He just stayed on his knees, with his eyes closed, praying.

The angels mixed up dough, put it in a pan and popped it in the oven. They put water on to boil and poured the beans in the pot. They cut up the cheeses and put them on a board. They put the oranges and apricots in a big bowl.

The friars could hear the pots and pans banging, the oven door opening and closing. Delicious smells floated out from under the kitchen door. They could hardly wait to eat.

Pascual felt a wing brush against his cheek. He opened his eyes.
There on the kitchen table was a feast fit for a friar!

That night, the friars ate everything Pascual put on their table.
"Pascual, your dinner was so good that you must be our cook forever!"

Poor Pascual! He didn't really want to be a cook. He wanted to help feed hungry people with the friars. But if they needed a cook, he would try. So the friars gave Pascual a Habit.

The next day, the angels came again. Pascual felt better. They cooked, and he prayed.

Day after day, tasty meals came from Pascual's kitchen.

How does he do it? the friars wondered.

But Pascual never said. The only one who knew was the kitchen cat.

Night after night, he told the friars that he wanted to help feed people. But they always said he was far too busy cooking for them to leave the monastery.

Finally, the friars had to know how Pascual cooked such delicious meals. So they peeked in and what a surprise! Pascual was praying, surrounded by angels stirring, slicing and baking.

"Pascual is so loved by God that He sends angels down to cook while Pascual prays," the friars said. "Imagine that!"

The friars never told Pascual that they knew his secret. But from then on, they took Pascual with them to feed the hungry.

And every once in a while, the friars would peek in and watch the angels flying all over the kitchen.

And Pascual? Well, he never ever learned how to cook even a cup
of beans!

Author's Note

PASCUAL is the patron saint of cooks and the kitchen. He is loved in Spain and Latin America, especially Mexico and New Mexico. He is often pictured wearing an apron and holding a wooden spoon and a bowl of beans. The kitchen cat is at his feet.

Born Pascual Bailón (Baylon) in May 1540 at Torre Hermosa, Aragon, Spain, he was a shepherd from ages seven to twenty-four. During those years, Pascual could be seen praying in the fields, singing to the sheep and weaving garlands of flowers for his sheep to wear. His pious nature was well known and even as a boy he had a strong devotion to the Holy Eucharist. So it came as no surprise when Pascual announced that he wanted to become a Franciscan with the friars of the Alcantrine Reform. His master tried to keep him home by offering Pascual an inheritance, but Pascual's mind was made up. He left for Valencia and applied for entry at the Franciscan monastery at Loreto.

But because Pascual was self-taught, the friars would only accept him as a lay brother. That meant he would spend his time doing the menial tasks around the monastery instead of preaching and feeding the poor. In fact, the first thing Pascual was ordered to do was to go to the kitchen and cook! Years later, Pascual admitted that he knew nothing about the kitchen. That is probably when the legend of the kitchen angels began.

Pascual Bailón died in May of 1592. He was proclaimed a saint in 1690 because of his life of prayer, humility and helping any who came to the kitchen door of the monastery.

TDEP — New Hampshire